AF493030

DRUGSTORE
DELIRIUM:

A "Humorous" Look At Retail Pharmacy

ACKNOWLEDGMENTS

*I wish to thank all those in my personal and
professional lives who made this book possible.*

Mr. Nick Productions, LLC

Copy Editor – R. Graham

Front cover art – Dr. Mayputz and Kristy Klein
Back cover and spine – Dr. Mayputz and Kristy Klein
Book layout – Kristy Klein / FifteenBlue.com

Photos of "typical" pharmacists – Anonymous
Published by Mr. Nick Productions, LLC ©2023

*This book was NOT written using
Artificial Intelligence or a ghostwriter*

ISBN: 979-8-218-14354-1

©2023. No portion of this book may be reproduced,
stored in a retrieval system, or transmitted in any form
or by any means, mechanical, recording or otherwise
without the written permission from the publisher.

Dedications

To my brilliant children, Brigette and Alex, who both wisely chose not to follow their parental units into pharmacy careers - or go into any health-related professions for that matter. In the one-word catchphrase of infamous WWE wrestling icon JBL: SMART!

And to my wonderful, beautiful and astute wife. You willingly slogged through a demanding and frequently demeaning pharmacy career to initially keep our young family afloat, and then uneventfully retired with dignity and grace. You led your professional vocation by example while simultaneously juggling many life-altering events, yet made every endeavor look effortless. Thank you.

Foreword

Most pill-pushing druggists have *funny* stories to share regarding their work-lives from behind the proverbial pharmacy counter. Some even put them down on paper. Although there are probably millions of amusing situations that have befallen our fellow comrades-in-arms, please join us as we relive a few of our own allegedly "humorous" tales while working as retail pharmacists.

Dr. I. Mayputz
Mrs. I. Mayputz

Preface

What is it about certain careers that make them easy to spoof and poke fun at? Podiatry, proctology, mortuary science, dentistry and, alas, pharmacy are but a few examples of professions that take it on the chin and suffer an unfair share of ignorant and sardonic abuse from the lay public. Is it the people populating those certain fields that make them easy targets of humorous derision or is it the jobs that lend themselves to unwarranted ridicule, regardless of who does them? Maybe both? Although many such vocations are scoffed at, they nevertheless seem to be in the upper echelon of monetary earnings, usefulness, and trustworthiness. I have had the pleasure, or displeasure, of being both a working pharmacist and dentist, though not at the same time. Pharmacy college, followed by dental school and a prosthodontic residency, consumed and then finished off my youthful and idealistic twenties. But as I recall, a pharmacy career had been a non-starter for me. That's why I left it in the first place, shortly after finishing pharmacy college and becoming duly licensed. Even during my brief but profound pre-graduation summer pharmacy internships, I had disquieted feelings of being treated as a worker bee, a sucker, someone to punch down at for not being fast enough, not possessing thorough knowledge about health insurances, or not readily giving unreasonable customers instant satisfaction. There were always problems that could not be remedied resulting in arguments and hard feelings, often among the pharmacy staff itself! Furthermore, a typical retail druggist is in an incredibly exposed and physically vulnerable position in most drugstores. Perhaps that is part of the reason why consumer vitriol can be so easily and intentionally lobbed at pharmacists and pharmacy in general. But some of those messed-up, firsthand pharmaceutical and ancillary experiences had bits of levity thrown in, resulting in comic family lore that has been passed down to our children and grandchildren by my retired pharmacist wife and me. Hopefully those same tales will be amusing to readers as well.

This is not my first bout in the squared circle of the writing realm. Some readers may have already indulged in my previous comic literary offerings and hopefully found them enjoyable. Although loosely based on my wife's and my work-related recollections and observations, this *pharmacy* book is "technically" fictional. It is a book of humor and should be taken as such. There is no malicious intent; the only intent is to entertain!

Dr. I. Mayputz

TABLE OF CONTENTS

Many people say that in addition to pills, capsules, ointments, and suppositories, laughter is the best medicine. However, the solemn places that dispense medicaments are often bereft of lively humor. Instead, the field of retail pharmacy can be fraught with stress, drudgery, exhaustion, unreasonable patient demands, and few bathroom breaks. Nevertheless, and no matter the typical arduous days involved, small snippets of amusement tend to sneak in now and again. To wit, I sought to highlight the "comedy" that often results in response to the juxtapositional situations and *controlled chaos* found in most pharmacy store settings. In any case, most names and places have been altered so as not to embarrass the guilty, berserk, bizarre, and downright scurvy. Hopefully you will find the stories within the following pages

to be humorous and you will laugh along with
me. Maybe at me, as well!

Enjoy.

Dr. I. Mayputz

1

Medical Arts

I had just finished pharmacy college, taken the board exams, and was actively looking for summertime employment near my hometown of Bumfuck, N.Y. prior to starting dental school in the fall. Meanwhile, Hottie Blondie, my former pharmacy college sweetheart and brand-new fiancée, was just starting her first summer internship in her daddy's drugstore in the central Adirondacks. It was the same store in which I gratefully interned the prior summer and where, under the facile mentorship of her knowledgeable and friendly father, I learned how to be a practical retail pharmacist. Hottie

Blondie was all set. But not me, as I searched high and low for a JOB! And then I remembered a particularly puny drugstore, one that I had passed many times in my youth. It was just past the two steep hills from my cow-infested and dusty village, in a small city where most of my fellow *country cousins* usually shopped. And that included my kinfolk, as well. I recalled the name of the pharmacy and decided to cold call the owner, using a traditional paper phone book to look up his number. After all, this was 1982: rotary telephones were de rigueur and phone numbers were still freely listed and publicly available. Anyhow, I called J.F. He answered and hastily explained that he was a one-man show and could not afford to hire another pharmacist. It was hard enough to keep his two male goofballs fully employed as it was, he further quipped. But before he put down the receiver, I piped up that I graduated from his alma mater and had also taken an archaic and obscure one semester course called Surgical Appliances. Well, that suddenly piqued his interest, and he politely let me keep on blabbing. I knew that his tiny drugstore was named Medical Arts Pharmacy for a reason. And the reason was that in addition to filling prescriptions, he and his two-man staff custom-measured, fitted, and sold surgical goods such as canes, colostomy bags, compression stockings, wheelchairs, trusses, etc. It was a dying but important medical art and niche business, yet here was a young, handsome - well, at least young - newly graduated pharmacist who not only had a rudimentary knowledge of that specific field but was interested in working for him. The next thing I knew, he had hired me over the phone and told me I would be working in tandem with his "specially trained morons;" each of whom could run the surgical part of the business. However, because I did not have my license yet, he stated that he would pay me less than a bona fide druggist's salary. Furthermore, he would cut out to play golf as much as possible, regardless of my lack of legal certification. I agreed; at least I had a place to work for three months. On the day we formally met, he scribbled down the golf club telephone number just in case of trouble, threw his gnarly clubs into the trunk of his black Lincoln Continental, and screeched out of the side driveway much like the Dynamic Duo with the Batmobile on their way to fight crime. The addled and quirky J.F. then proceeded to ILLEGALLY leave me alone for days on end (I wasn't yet officially licensed) while placing me under the alleged tutelage of the gruesome twosome: Limbo Jimbo and old man Scurvy. Neither were druggists but could supposedly "help" me out in a pinch behind the counter if needed. They were both local characters, knew all the loyal patients, and were old veterans of the pharmacy game. Come to think of it, I never knew their real first or last names. I guess I never asked. Nonetheless, it turned out to be a fun summer. I filled the sporadic and uncomplicated prescriptions and sold the odd over-the-counter products like tick-removal combs, rat traps, anti-dandruff shampoos, and motor oil. But I was mostly immersed in the surgical trade. On some weekdays, Scurvy had two fitting rooms going at once while Limbo Jimbo manned the pharmacy cash register next to the antiquated drug bench. Of course, I was called in to assist Scurvy on many occasions and quickly became well-acquainted with crutches, orthopedic knee braces, post breast cancer bras, etc. Both sexes trusted us to correctly, unashamedly, and non-judgmentally fit them with the proper devices and apparatus. In retrospect, I had never touched so many little old ladies in intimate places before in my entire young life. I routinely do that now, but it's MY old lady, so…. Nevertheless, who knew that pharmacy could be so fascinating and life-changing? And the owner? He played endless rounds of golf with a greenhorn at the helm of his mini pharmaceutical emporium. Good for him! Hopefully I had been a worthy hire.

2

Mainstain

Okay, I added the s in the title because that made-up word sort of applies to this tale. It was the hot summer of 1983, and I was available for some easy lifting after completing a strenuous first year of dental school. And what better way to use my dormant pharmacy license than to effortlessly earn some cashola at my future father-in-law's drugstore when he decided to go on a lengthy summertime vacation. Meanwhile my betrothed bride-to-be was working her second consecutive summer of a mandatory pharmacy internship, although this time not in her dad's apothecary. Instead, she was employed at the VA hospital near our old pharmacy college in a highly coveted position which I had "saved" for her. I had "talked" to the chief of the pharmacy service before departing and implored him to hire Hottie Blondie when she applied for her internship there. It's all who you know! In any event, I drove up north alone. Then her mom and pop took off to Greece, leaving me and two reliable clerks behind to mind the pharmacy and hopefully, not kill anyone. The store was in the bowels of the Adirondack mountains, up in the sticks, yet had an excellent location on Main Street. It was open nine to nine, six days a week, and was always very busy. Those were long days, but I was making decent coin and did not complain. However, it

was during the late-night hours that
things got a little rambunctious and out
of control. Middle-aged assistant Irene
would depart at five p.m., leaving a
burly highschooler to help me until
closing time. Big John S. was working
there because he was the teenaged son
of close family friends and could be
trusted. Plus, it was good to have a
hulking presence in the store just in
case of late-night trouble. I mean,
people can get drunk, high, and
belligerent even in a small, no-account
village, one that had more black bears
than humans. Anyway, the local, one-
reel movie theater was close by and
always caused an influx of rowdy kids
to come slamming through the door to
purchase candy and condoms before
the shows on Friday and Saturday

nights. Technically, anyone of any age could purchase prophylactics, but they were kept inside a glass case and needed to be asked for. Well, this always caused great consternation and embarrassment for the adolescents and that's where John came in. No one wanted to ask me; I was the adult in the room. But John was popular and *cool* and would often be slipped some greenbacks for a pack of Trojans; in turn he would then routinely and surreptitiously procure the rubbers for the awkward teenagers. I knew what was transpiring but said nothing, as long as the money eventually made it into the cash box. And it did. But one raucous Friday night turned out a bit differently. With a store full of sexually tense teens browsing and loudly chattering, an

attractive middle-aged lady came up to
the till amid all the noise and plopped a
large tube of cream on the counter. She
grinned widely and I noticed her
"perfect" teeth. After all, I was a dental
student and appreciated her pearly
whites. And while John was supposedly
dealing with his buds and all the
giggling girls, I walked over a few steps
to the cash register to help her check
out. I immediately saw that she wanted
to purchase something called Maintain.
Being in somewhat of a silly mood
because of all the youthful energy in the
store, I glibly and suggestively started
counseling her without thinking twice.
I assumed she was smiling from ear to
ear because of what was going to take
place in her life later that night. I
laughingly told her that only a small

amount of the agent had to be smeared on the head, that it took about 20 minutes to start working, that hands had to be thoroughly washed after its messy application and that it might stain clothing. And then I stood there with a knowing smirk on my face not realizing that John had overheard every word I said. "But I just had my teeth bleached by the dentist. Will this toothpaste help me to MAINTAIN my smile?" she blurted out, looking a bit confused because of my previous explanation and warnings. Now it was my turn to appear nonplussed while trying to keep a straight face. I thought she knew what she was about to purchase and froze in horror for sounding so blatantly and sexually condescending. Meanwhile, John had excused himself and went into the back room from whence I heard uncontrollable shrieks and howls, ones that would not stop. The lady started to get the gist that something was amiss and nervously begged me to ring her up so she could leave. Meanwhile, the line of yelling, young buyers behind her had grown and I started to groan. I leaned over to her and whispered that Maintain was not a toothpaste, but a topical numbing cream used to treat premature ejaculation. Her winsome, toothy façade faded, she became visibly irate and then brusquely marched out of the drugstore, as I quickly secreted the "offending cream" under the counter. John was still nowhere to be found but his laughter continued unabated. I felt so embarrassed for that woman as I cashed out the remaining kids and forcefully called for John to come out of hiding. He finally emerged with a tear-stained, reddened face and appeared very disheveled. Hard guffawing will do that to you. He knew about Maintain and could not contain himself, hence his abrupt departure from his post in front of that woman. I looked at him and he started that apoplectic chuckling again. Finally, I asked him if he was responsible for stocking that cream in the wrong spot. After a long pause, and in between snorts and wheezes, he managed to say that Irene had done it. The next day I confronted Irene, who had worked in the pharmacy for close to twenty years. I asked if she had placed that certain object in the dental products section.

"Of course I did. That's where toothpaste belongs," she bluntly shot back, as if I had accused her of not knowing her job. When I explained that it was a new material and what its purpose was, she had no visible reaction and admonished me for picking on her. She wasn't ruffled in the least and then accused my future father-in-law of being a pervert and for selling that "junk" in the first place. Wowzers, she had maintained her composure as I just shook my head and got back to filling prescriptions. But then I wondered, who was REALLY *cool* under fire, Irene or John?

3

Nothing Doing

The summer of 1983 found me
working as a substitute druggist in place
of my vacationing future father-in-law
at his corner drugstore in the
Adirondacks. It was a beautiful
pharmacy with the long-defunct soda
fountain and high-rise swivel-chairs still
lining the back wall. It was a great place
of employment; slow enough to
properly address the pharmaceutical
concerns of the village people, yet active
enough to make a good living. And
there I was, ensconced behind the
"bench" as the able replacement for Joe,
the store's popular owner. Most of the
local populace had known of my arrival

and enthusiastically welcomed me as a quasi-family member. After all, I was engaged to Joe's Hotsy-Totsy eldest daughter who would also be a druggist quite soon. Even so, I was really there because of nepotism. And, why not? Why hire an unknown *nebbish* as a relief pharmacist when Joe could have his trusted future son-in-law manning the store and the all-important cash register? And that's why I was there. A win-win scenario for everyone concerned. However, I had not worked since the summer of '82 because I was currently a dental student. But the memories and triple threat wave of capsule-counting, consulting, and cashing-out quickly came rushing at me and I was effectively back in the retail saddle again! But it was all good as I began a lengthy stint in the drugstore. Friendly locals would come and go, and some would stop by to idly *kibbitz*, and check to make sure I was doing alright. You know, nice folks that were looking out for me, on behalf of their beloved Joe. And I greatly appreciated it. However, as the days went along, I couldn't help but notice that even though people were polite and deferential to me, there seemed to be a palpable pall in the air - an overall mood of resignation. Now, I am no psychologist, but even I could tell that something was slightly askew. Maybe it was caused by the depleted ozone layer, acid rain, mountain smog, or something else that resulted in a noticeable mental malaise of the hard-working populace in a hard-scrabble part of the state. But then I noticed the prescriptions that were being filled. Many older men were on old-fashioned, impotence-inducing, anti-hypertensive drugs (such as Aldomet) while many adult women were on libido-busting benzodiazepines (such as Valium). And I'm sure there was nightly consumption of alcohol by both sexes as well. Add that all together and you get a toxic mix of flaccidity and ambivalence resulting in less nooky. There was nothing doing in town, if you know what I mean. Now, I know I am just generalizing and did not do a scientific study, however, suffice it to say that things clearly changed when Viagra hit the market in 1989. My father-in-law told me later that he could not keep enough supply of that new drug on his shelf, such was the great initial demand. On many occasions he illegally doled it out to his closest buddies, one precious pill at a time, as "free therapeutic samples." So, there it is, my flippant societal observation in '83 that was seemingly rectified by the late eighties. However, I'm not sure if all the stressed-out, heterosexual ladies appreciated the penile awakenings all around them. But who knows, perhaps many did.

4

Bank Teller or Druggist?

Even to the discerning observer, sometimes it is hard to tell the difference between a bank teller and a pharmacist. Sure, the jobs are obviously and vastly different. However, when it comes time to engage the lay public, the professions tend to converge, at least in the rancor, bewilderment, and confusion that often result as consequences of the verbal interactions. Let me further explain: How many times have you stood in a long, non-moving bank line and been privy to the conversation going on between a patron and the teller? Probably many times. Often it goes something like this: "It's my mother's account and I just want to withdraw some cash to cover my stepsister's bail; she's in the slammer again." "Do you have an account with us?" "No, but the last names are the same so it should be no problem." "No, it is a problem and only your mom can withdraw money unless you have a joint account with her." "Oh, maybe I do but I forgot my bank card and pin number. Anyway, just give me the bills in hundreds…." And that was just the tip of the iceberg of a lengthy and maddening exchange that almost always ends by the manager's involvement, the person leaving in disgust or eventually being assisted by an ASSociate in the sequestered foyer of the bank. Wouldn't it be nice to have a special line solely dedicated to "those people who invent banking as per their own logic" and queues for the rest of us that "know what we're doing?" Of course, but alas, at the pharmacy consultation window, an eerily similar convo can take place: "Can I pay for a few oxycontin pills to tide me over until my insurance kicks in next month? And then it will cover all of it in full. What do you mean you can't give it to me? I have an old prescription for it, don't I? What do you mean a new prescription is needed? Look, I'm in pain. Can't you just phone my stupid doctor and straighten it out? I don't know if she works on Saturdays or if the damn clinic is even open. No, my drug plan is not expired; it's just in my fuckin' ex-husband's name. I'll just wait here while you call." Wouldn't it be nice to have a large sign posted next to

the pharmacy department that listed
the dos and don'ts of dispensing? I
mean, come on. Even during my very
brief pharmacy tenure, I dealt with
hundreds of situations that were most
likely commonsense to the asking
patient but did not follow the
prescribed protocols of pharmacy
practice. Furthermore, it was very
stressful trying vainly to explain
exorbitant co-pays, lack of insurance
coverage for certain medicines, and why
inexpensive generics were not available
for all name-brand drugs. To the
exasperated patient it often appeared as
a gotcha game with the pharmacist
concocting lame excuses or feigning
indifference. To the frustrated druggist,
it was a lose-lose situation often
exacerbated by recalcitrant prescribers,

incompetent insurance company personnel, patient ignorance, and sometimes, idiocy on all fronts. All in all, the misunderstandings and miscommunications were commonplace yet bothersome. But it was no one's fault. How could patients possibly know all the laws, rules, and regulations governing pharmacy? Similarly, how could customers possibly know all the laws, rules, and regulations governing banking? There's just got to be a better way forward in both professions, even with today's seemingly "easy" online drug and banking transactions. For even they sometimes go awry and need live human intervention.

5

The Usual

I'm sure most frontline retail druggists have amusing stories to share regarding patients and their pharmacy faux pas. You know, the kind of tales involving ignorance of medicaments, placing drugs into unusual orifices, misinterpreting doctors' rushed ramblings as well as confusing pharmacists' convoluted consultations. You know, the "usual" crap that sometimes happens at the fucked-up intersection of medicine delivery and usage. And that unfortunate verbal dysfunctional junction is often the crux of the problem. Whether at the physician's office or the drugstore, the practitioner's skill of properly informing the patient can be the difference between efficacious therapy and sticking suppositories up the ass without unwrapping them from the foil packaging first. You know, little details like that; important facts that a disgruntled patient would say were never fully explained. And this was way before DIY YouTube videos could be studied and emulated. Back in the day, dictating doctors and dispensing druggists had to be on their respective games in order for patients NOT to get "hurt." And that was always the case whenever I manned the pharmacy counter. "Hey, Doc, the quack-doctor at the fuckin' health center told me to take baby aspirin for my old ticker. Is that right? Or is it for my baby grandchild?" Oh, boy. "Hey, Doc, are the adult diapers for grown-up kids with a problem?" Well, not exactly. "Excuse me, Mr. Pharmacist, do you stick the penicillin tablets in the earholes before or after the earache drops go in?" Please, make them all stop! Anyway, those kinds of queries and my often-amusing responses were mostly considered mild and comic briefings, and no one was medicinally injured. Unfortunately, there were also "stories" of people who were not appropriately educated and the resultant dire consequences that transpired. Patients could become seriously ill due to incorrect dosing, the faulty timing involved when popping prescription pills as well as from the improper usage of medical devices.

Pharmaceuticals and medicament-delivery agents such as syringes, needles, and glass ampules can be outright dangerous if not taken as directed or misused, respectively. Pharmacists are usually the last informational stop on the highway of health, so to speak. Hopefully, most retail druggists are personal enough to speak up to make darn sure that the counted capsules are consumed correctly. I always did, whether patients wanted to hear my spiel or not. I even obnoxiously spoke up when seemingly non-lethal, over-the-counter products were purchased. Again, many allegedly "humorous" incidents can occur after the brief verbiage exchanged between doctor and patient and pharmacist and patient. Some outcomes can be truly

comical for all parties involved,
however, some results of simple
misunderstandings can become
malpractice-inducing or downright
deadly.

6

A Cultural Awakening

She didn't move to the Rotten Apple by choice; no freakin' way. But love had gotten the best of her, and Hottie Blondie effectively became a victim of circumstance. Her future husband was a second-year dental student in the big city and a long-distance marriage was unappealing. So, after the June nuptials at the Big Moose Chapel, in Big Moose, N.Y., she packed up her meager belongings and trekked south to join him in a vermin-invaded, third story walk-up apartment on 10th Avenue and 25th Street, right in the heart of the gay section called Chelsea. And although she had experienced some of the highlights and lowlights of small city living while studying pharmacy in Smallbany, N.Y., nothing had adequately prepared her for the psychological "abuse" she would unwittingly endure while existing in a mostly derelict metropolis. But besides the crime, grime, and bustle that were foisted on her daily, there were the masses of asses she had to contend with. Most were not like the kindly mountain peddlers and harmless hillbillies of her hometown, nor did they resemble the pretentious people in the state's capitol who fancied themselves urbane. In fact, many were actual *perps* that she would soon be communicating with not only at work, but during everyday interactions in the concrete jungle. However, she spent the first few weeks unemployed and, along with her new husband, canvassed the city as a wide-eyed tourist. Together they slowly but surely started to experience an oftentimes overwhelming environment. The rest of their "story" is rather mundane – smalltown girl and boy successfully negotiate a humongous town regardless of all the "strange" bullshit thrown at them…. But as stated previously, there is one thing that bears repeating: Not being a natural-born Doubting Thomas like her husband, Hottie Blondie was oftentimes amazed at how true-to-form certain human behaviors tended to be along ethnic, racial, and religious lines. I mean, she was worldly to a point, yet kept getting buffaloed now and again. She was frequently surprised by people and their typecast characteristics, ones that she used to laugh off as being untrue, until she witnessed them firsthand. And working in a hurried, metropolitan chain drugstore with the diaspora she serviced only compounded her "cultural education." But she survived, although now she knew to walk in backwards at an Orthodox Jewish wedding reception. And the top-hatted, black-clad Hasidim were not on their way to fancy dress parties. She learned to stay away from Harlem and to get out of ALL parks at sundown, before the criminal element went to work. And homeless sidewalk buskers were real, as were the bedraggled male street flashers who also sold loose joints in small bags. Disheveled panhandlers in the subway stations begged for jingling change and drunken bums galore graced most every nook and cranny, always on the look-out for handouts. In addition to noticeable archetypal behaviors, such as smooth-talking and suave-acting Italian men and sexily attired LatinX women who played up to their respective stereotypes, there also were the plain-Jane, buttoned-up and short-bobbed female workers of the '80s, who wore power-walking sneakers while clutching stilettos. Anyway, Hottie Blondie unintentionally observed numerous examples of extreme dichotomy in a seemingly vibrant city that never slept. There was war and peace - and love and hate - all at the same time and always around her. As a physically and mentally overworked druggist she often

confided in her husband that
unfortunately he was mostly correct in
his assessment of city-dwellers and
admitted that she had a way to go to
catch up to his level of healthy
skepticism, albeit with a hint of
cynicism thrown in. However, he did
have a two-year head start....

7

Getting Started

Oh boy, this was it. Big city life and Hottie Blondie getting started as a licensed and salaried pharmacist for a chain drugstore on East 70th Street. It was a mere bus ride and then a short walk away from 10th Avenue, where she and I lived. My Upstate New York wife was well educated and well trained as a druggist. Unfortunately, all that copious studying, book learning and wherewithal did her little good when faced with introductory adversity such as Howard H., her first co-worker and boss. My, he was extremely rotund and had a certain maleficence about him. A double whammy of a grossly overweight druggist struggling to be a reasonable human being. What the hell? Hottie Blondie not only had to initially survive the sordid city but oxymoronic and obnoxious Howard as well. And, yes, her first day turned out to be a real beaut! It was early morn but before she could even finish putting her coat and homemade lunch away, Howard started right in. He hollered that there was a new pharmacist on board and that he would be training her up. As the rest of the supplicant team gathered, he took it upon himself to introduce my wife and to growl more than a few syllables. At bottom, Howard was in charge. He was the unmarried, vane, middle-aged ringleader of a certifiable circus with a menagerie of attractive women masquerading as competent support staff. But Hottie Blondie's initial undoing was her sensitive sense of smell. It seems that Howard had a ridiculous, slicked-back comb-over going on and used a stinky pomade to keep it in place. It stunk up the whole store bigtime; even the back corners of the pharmacy department reeked of that cheap hair gel. It was that bad, and my wife started to feel a bit queasy. With the stench permeating the air, he opened his pie hole once again and continued his verbal assault. Loud, self-righteous, and bigoted, he claimed that he was a Yiddish product of the Flatbush section in Queens. He added that he couldn't help being himself as he gestured to her, the cowering newbie, and bellowed, "I will teach you to be a REAL pharmacist, and these girls will assist you." And then he emphatically said, "Forget about all you learned in school. This is where REAL pharmacy begins and ends. I can take a homeless hobo off the streets and make him a druggist in ONE day. To be a two-bit pharmacist, all you have to do is look, listen, and be careful, period!" And with that statement he finished boasting for a moment, but kept pointing a fat, accusatory finger at my wife, who was thoroughly flabbergasted. She was scared by all the pontificating done by this short, pudgy and pugnacious blowhard but felt compelled to ask a few questions anyway. "What about the compounding part?" she meekly implored. "We don't do that here. We send those prescriptions down the street to that private mom-and-pop drugstore.

Those assholes have the time to do that kind of shit," he yelled. "And what about counseling patients?" my wife blurted out. At this point a panting and grunting Howard turned beet-red. "You can read, can't you?" he spewed out while glaring at my startled wife. "When jerks ask you dumbass questions, you rip the patient package insert (PPI) off the pill bottle and read the 'patient' part to them. You know, side effects, etc. It's all right there, in plain English," he sputtered. (Nowadays, a pharmacist can easily check about a product on the computer. In those days the computers were not as sophisticated, and the PPI was an invaluable and quick source of info for the pharmacist). My wife was trembling slightly as the staff members took their places. The store was about to officially open that morning and she hoped and prayed that things would go smoothly. Hottie Blondie recalled what Howard had just said and remembered her halcyon college days and limited dispensing experience. She had also worked in her father's small drugstore as an intern and learned a thing or two about the moral aspects of pharmacy and the ethical treatment of sick customers. She wondered if she could stomach this kind of maniacal and cynical approach to the distribution of vital medicaments to ill patients. And as she scanned the pretty workforce, she also got the uneasy feeling that they were not overly friendly and were basically dolled-up city gals who looked out for number one. Suddenly, Howard glanced at my wife, who stood a foot taller than he, and smiled an evil grin. It was showtime and time for her to start learning the ropes. And learn she did, the school-of-hard-knocks way, the Howard way. However, she and I both had it bad and that early period in our marriage tested our resolve to stay spliced and not to panic and bail on each other, or on our chosen professions. Things were not copacetic at all, but together we gave it the "old college try" and just barely made it to the future. At the time, I was toiling away in my third year of dental school while Hottie Blondie slaved away in a pressure-filled drugstore with the added discomfort of dealing with a largely dysfunctional pharmacy faction. Because even though the female pharmacy technicians and clerks were somewhat helpful, their dour dispositions and chattiness got under her skin. Most days were difficult for my wife as she tried to keep her sanity and humanity intact while interacting with them. And then there was gruff and cantankerous Howard to contend with – the literal elephant in the room. He continually plowed through life with bluster and bravado and took no prisoners. But she did become efficient, fast, accurate and responsible, and Howard and his constant barking most likely had something to do with it. Fast forwarding a few years found my wife working for the same chain outfit but with a different pharmacy manager and at a new location. This drugstore was just as ridiculously busy but had a nicer boss and healthier mental vibe going on. Anyway, one day a stranger appeared at her counter, leaned up and uttered a timid greeting. "Do I know you? Are you a patient of ours?" asked my wife while staring down at the svelte, balding, neatly dressed and reserved gentleman. "It's me, Howard," the man answered in a cheerful manner. "No fuckin' way," thought Hottie Blondie as she dropped what she was doing and continued to gaze at him. But then she realized it really was Howard H. and enthusiastically invited him to join her behind the bench for a quick chinwag. He responded positively to her overture and appeared delighted for a chance at some enjoyable social intercourse and perhaps to bury the hatchet. He told her that he was in the neighborhood and stopped by because he knew she worked there. And all this time she thought that he had summarily despised her. He added that he had lost over one hundred pounds of weight and appreciated life so much more. He continued with more conciliatory and genteel chit chat while my transfixed wife raptly listened. "What a transformation," she murmured to herself as a relaxed Howard kept on talking in a soothing cadence. Completely absent was the repulsive pit bull persona. In its place stood a "new" man; a newly minted and decent man who seemed eager to make amends and reconnect with fellow humans. The inner demons that had certainly dogged him were apparently gone. And he seemed to willingly accept his balding pate too, without resorting to the smelly, hair-care bullshit of yesteryear. He went on to tell her that he was still employed by the same chain company as she. And when the brief visit was over, she sincerely thanked him for coming in. It had markedly brightened her dull day and, hopefully, his as well. I recall her recounting this story later that evening and she seemed to get genuine closure from an unspeakably volatile time in her nascent career. And most of it had been caused by the low self-esteem and defensiveness of one individual. Although now, after working for a few years, she better understood how the taxing and exacting world of retail pharmacy could have contributed to Howard's mental turbulence and unhappiness.

8

Daily Drama

The title is basically self-explanatory and, in this instance, it does not refer to pharmacist-patient interactions. Rather, it is only a slight exaggeration of the interplay that took place between staff members in a ferociously fast-paced retail chain drugstore. Though not religious, Catholic-raised Hottie Blondie would sometimes recall the Christian devotional prayer "Give Us This Day Our Daily Bread" and sarcastically substitute the word bread with the word drama as she entered her workplace on East 70th Street. But it was not the expected squabbling and squawking of a normal family. Digging deeper, she realized that her partner-pharmacist, technicians, assistants, intern, and clerks were from differing countries, races, cultures, and upbringings with disparate viewpoints on everything in life. Starting off, and as previously mentioned, Howard H. was her working partner and pharmacy boss, and a deviant piece of work - enough said. However, my wife was begrudgingly okay with his particular paradigm and peccadilloes. But her female support staff, in lieu of being supportive, instead chose to vociferously share their unfiltered grievances on various subjects including love, relationships, marriage, and sex out loud and in the open, and often within earshot of paying customers. What the eff? Hottie Blondie had a busy drug counter to run and yet the jabbering gals were engaged in more gossipy griping than laboring. And although "tea spilling" occurred regularly, my wife always took great care not to prejudge or assume anything deleterious about anyone's outward character or background. She was a good listener, observer, and a quick learner. However, some of the things that transpired around her could not be unheard, unseen, or unlearned: Pretty assistant May Ling, born in Myanmar (Burma), often bragged about her marriage to a Yiddish fellow who taught English to newly arrived, legal immigrants. Of course, she must have been a very willing student during his evening lectures and obviously got a rise out of him; most likely before, during, and after class! She considered it a major coup to now be officially considered Jew-ish. "Better married to a Jew than a chauvinistic Burmese," she would boastfully crow. Then there was Lilly Li, a frequent substitute pharmacist at the drugstore. She originally hailed from Wuhan and was a consummate sourpuss. And although alluring, perhaps being short and visibly pregnant contributed to her guarded and icy persona. But maybe there was more to it? One day Hottie Blondie nonchalantly motioned to Lilly and enthusiastically stated that she looked great and asked if she was excited about having a baby. Well, that turned out to be a big mistake. In broken English Lilly exclaimed, "No, no, no, not good, not happy!" My wife gave her a blank stare as Lilly continued, "Only good thing about pregnant is no sex with no good HUBBAND. After having baby, I stay home with HIM, and more BAD sex." Oops. Then Hottie Blondie put her foot in her mouth once again. "Why did you get married in the first place if you were not attracted to him?" she innocently queried. "Arranged marriage; stupid father not choose well!" Lilly wailed. My exasperated wife nodded sympathetically but inadvertently opened up a never-ending dialogue of resentment and capitulation that she felt obligated to hear out whenever Lilly worked in her store. Gee whiz, all because of Hottie Blondie's empathy…. Narda was a prima donna princess pharmacy tech who thought she was above everyone else. She lived with her parents and spent most of her income on designer-clothes, jewelry, and makeup. She constantly bragged about being engaged to a White, "superior" man, who was an engineer. Because of her LatinX accent and brownish complexion, my wife casually asked her where she originally came from. "Well, I'm definitely NOT from Puerto Rico," she angrily chided, as if Hottie Blondie had blatantly accused her of some grievous indiscretion. "I'm Dominican and don't you EVER call me Puerto Rican," she further snarled, while my wife just stood there with her mouth open. Meanwhile, Nia, a good-looking, young, and pleasant Puerto Rican clerk had overheard everything, and also just stood there with her mouth agape. Anyway, that's how the

"Nia and Narda" shitshow began with escalating petty jealousies between the two that usually ended with verbal volleys involving cultural innuendoes being hurled at one another. But that kind of juvenile brinkmanship frequently made Hottie Blondie cross. How dare those two make her days even more downhearted than they already were? And then she thought of the rest of the catty female crew and the resultant boisterous bitterness that exited their respective pie holes and then subsequently entered her unwilling earholes. It was all so unnecessary. But wait a second, her other senses took a beating as well. As already explained, the Americanized women workers were from other nations and, as if to prove a point, they oftentimes flaunted their homespun tendencies in the open. For example, the wealthy and condescending pharmacy intern purposefully wore pungent, eye-watering perfume and outlandish clothing from her former homeland. And to make matters worse, while very cheerful and personable, she was not very bright. All in all, it was quite a rude awakening for Hottie Blondie, what with the unexpected avalanche of strange smells, sights, and sounds as well as the episodes of incompetence exhibited. And not to mention the plethora of contrasting, clashing, and often combative personalities that she was forced to skillfully navigate through. With the pharmacy department atmosphere already simmering like the innards of a highly charged pressure-cooker, she really didn't need the added aggravation of having her sensitive senses and intellect so insulted. Oh, well, it was all part and parcel of the *normative* daily drama, I'm afraid.

9

Can't Unsee It

It was autumn and a substitute pharmacist would be working with my wife at her drugstore on East 86th Street for a few days. It was common practice to shuttle druggists around as needed between the chain-owned stores to cover for illnesses, vacations, etc. Hottie Blondie also participated in the practice. Anyway, the day arrived, and Randy showed up right on time and ready to work. Since it was an insanely hectic store, they would be functioning in tandem throughout the day. My wife graciously welcomed him to "her" store, and they got busy – not sexually, but filling prescriptions. Randy was newly licensed, White, slightly built, wore glasses, had stylized short hair, and was demonstrably on the quiet side. No outbursts, mutterings, or swear words came out of his mustachioed mouth. He had that Freddie Mercury-type handle-bar mustache that was popular in the gay community in the '80s, but so did lots of straight men at the time, and Hottie Blondie thought nothing of it. I mean her own father sported sideburns and a mustache for the first time after being a lifelong, clean-cut, conservative druggist. Even my reserved, tenured-professor father ditched his handsome baby face with the addition of thick facial hair under his nose, as if to finally buck "authority." However, as chairman of the engineering department at his college, he WAS the authority. Oh, well. Of course, when I had hippie-inspired long hair in the late '70s he often had choice, harsh words for me. Now at long last he seemed to finally embrace his wild, "beatnik" side. But he was a decade too late, and it made me laugh. Anyhow, Randy and my wife had gotten along famously, and she was truly sorry to see him leave. There were no cross words exchanged betwixt them and the workplace flow had been smooth. She admired his even-toned counseling skills with pushy patients and marveled at his seemingly non-liberal ideology at such a young age. What was not to like? He was an all-around great guy and one diligent druggist! For subsequent weeks my wife would mention his name now and then, but life went on and Randy soon became an afterthought. However, one fateful Friday night we decided to go out to our favorite Chinese restaurant called The Chelsea Big Wok. We donned light jackets and began our short stroll to the well-known Asian eatery on lower 10th Avenue. Hottie Blondie and I figured this was the perfect way to end a daunting week while dining on haute Hunan cuisine. Romantically holding hands, we walked slowly down the street and saw a couple approaching us at a fast clip. It wasn't an unusual sight because the city was always chock-full of pedestrians that hoofed it everywhere. Meanwhile, yellow taxicabs buzzed all around like bees, but powerwalking to various destinations was all the rage at the time.

Anyway, as the aforementioned couple approached, we could make out that they were both men, one old and stout, and the other youthful and slender. Both were decked out in heavy, black leather gear, complete with biker-type chain accessories, spiked collars, boots, caps, and gloves. It wasn't Halloween, so they stuck out a bit in the late evening light. But maybe they were going to a costume party dressed as Rob Halford of Judas Priest? Of course, why not? After all, it was the city which never slept and where the abnormal was frequently the norm. Now that the quickly walking couple was upon us, my wife looked up and exclaimed, "Randy, Randy, is that you?" The younger partner of the twosome quickly looked down at the stone sidewalk as he brushed past her and did not utter a single word of acknowledgement. Hottie Blondie spun on her high heel and once more futilely shouted his name into the looming darkness as they hurriedly disappeared from view. It really was Randy, wasn't it? For a brief instant she was unsure and appeared puzzled at his apparent embarrassment and rudeness. But then it dawned on her that her excellent vision had not deceived her. It HAD been Randy all along and he and his male "pal" more than likely dressed like that as part of their *normal*, after-hours, hedonistic lifestyle. Nevertheless, she was astonished by his brazen, S & M-inspired, non-druggist attire just as he had probably been mortified to be seen by her in public. He must have thought that with eight million people living in the city, what were the odds of literally running into a heterosexual workmate who also happened to live in that same hotbed of homosexuality called the Chelsea District? Well, the chances were miniscule, to say the least. But it happened, nonetheless. Suffice it to say that our dinner conversation that evening was very lively. While on our way home, Hottie Blondie was still amazed at seeing Randy in all his decadent finery yet was hurt that he had not stopped to chat. She stated that she was open-minded and never would have divulged his "secret identity." However, perhaps he had not fully recognized her that night because she was clothed in a little black dress and black stockings, with black gloves and

four-inch-tall black pumps to boot. Fair
enough.

10

In Through the Back Door

Newly married and still a relatively newly minted pharmacist, my wife was living in a big city and managing to cope with working for a major chain drugstore. She wasn't overtly naïve, but neither was she being radicalized into a serial cynic. At least not yet. R.K. was her new brash, married-with-children boss and pharmacist co-worker, whose long daily shifts overlapped with Hottie Blondie's at the East 86th Street drugstore. He "knew-it-all" and enjoyed spouting off about his supposed "street cred" as a wise but misanthropic druggist. By contrast, my kind and thoughtful wife was happy just to be employed at this new store and away from the previous rabid "zoo" on East 70th Street. Initially, however, she did not catch on to the twisted-thinking populace that lurked around this location as well. One day, she answered the phone and innocently and professionally proceeded to counsel a man as to the proper usage of an enema. As R.K. listened in, she carefully and gently went through the physical steps necessary to produce the desired outcome. "But how do I put the tube in?" the man on the phone asked. Well, that elicited some more supportive but suggestive-sounding words from my consulting wife. "And how does it feel when it goes in?" he then asked in a breathless voice. She told him there would be fullness due to the expanding rectum being filled with the medicinal fluid. At that point R.K. started chuckling which caused her to suddenly stop the conversation mid-sentence. Was the guy on the other end a pervert and getting free phone sex from her? You think? She was no patsy and angrily slammed down the receiver. Then she glared at her boss, who by now was laughing hysterically. But things did not stop there. That man called again and again. Each time my wife would hang up the phone. Sometimes R.K. would pick up the receiver, glance mischievously at my wife, and obnoxiously announce, "The enema-man wants you to tell him where to stick it." The creepy caller must have known what my pretty wife looked like and where she worked.

Anyway, those phony shenanigans went on for a while but finally ceased. In the end, Hottie Blondie got an unwarranted and unwilling "education." Hopefully that man got all his probing questions answered somewhere else.

11

Stepping Out and Stepping Over

Naturally, Hottie Blondie had to dress the part when heading to work. That and the requisite make-up which she dutifully applied prior to exiting our new, second story, two-bedroom, rental flat in the safe, quiet, Mafia-patrolled, Glendale area of Queens. I mean, she was the druggist behind the pharmacy counter first seen by customers; she had to project a certain respectable, put-together, clean, care-giver image and she did not disappoint. But getting to the store was another matter. Although we now had my old college-era jalopy, the crappy city parking situation and hellacious drive stopped us from using it on most weekdays. And like that over-the-top 1987 comic film *Planes, Trains and Automobiles*, my wife's daily *gauntlet-run* from our rented place in Queens to the very core of the Rotten Apple required using various modes of transportation. Those trips included paranoid vigilance to hopefully avoid any would-be threatening situations. And on this day, after standing on the fecal-stinking bus and then strap-hanging and swaying back and forth on three different urine-soaked, graffiti-laden, subway trains, she finally arrived safely at her latest place of employment on East 86th Street. Yay – but just in time to find a bevy of somber city cops carting away a tarp-covered homicide victim who had been murdered in the wee hours of the morning right in front of the pharmacy's door. As the residual blood was being hosed off the sidewalk by numb city workers, a kind officer grabbed her by the elbow and effectively guided her to step over the crime scene before she entered the store. It was all so surreal and yet, so routine and real. No one said a word as all the people involved played their respective parts. They behaved as if seasoned actors in a silent, chronologically choreographed movie - from the perpetrator to the deceased, then to the law and clean-up committee, and on down to the attractive, blonde, female lead. But this was not a celluloid horror flick, and the gunman was still at large, at least that's what the po-po mumbled. My wife was still visibly shaking and distraught when she took her elevated place behind the pharmacy bench as the first annoying customers started right in, peppering her with crapola. You know, the usual non-stop barrage of medical questions and drug problems that she could not readily answer or solve, especially after her earlier shocking ordeal. But she persevered, as she had done countless times before, put on a brave face, and braved the rest of the day head on. As a former tough Adirondack-mountain girl, she did not let a typical common city killing (the 1980s were notorious for huge spikes in crime in most large cities) hinder her psychologically. It was to be expected. She was actually surprised she hadn't yet witnessed multiple murders a day up to that point. Anyway, she fought back the urge to crumple or quit under such soul-sucking circumstances, finished her demanding twelve-hour shift, and matter-of-factly took the same dangerous subway trains and buses home, but in reverse order from the morning commute. I took the exact same means of transport but in a slightly different direction because of a different destination – a dental residency program at a major VA hospital. I, too, weathered similarly menacing and odorous back and forth journeys. Fortunately, nothing injurious or murderous befell either of us during the rest of our time in that voluntary purgatory. Amen.

12

Lunch Time!

On most days she brown-bagged it. However, once in a while, my wife and some of her female drugstore co-workers would surreptitiously scamper out from behind the pharmacy counter to get a quick bite to eat. It wasn't a strenuous walk, and they weren't gone for very long. For they were always stupidly busy and there was no official time-period allotted for "pharmacy slaves" to rejuvenate their brains with needed nourishment. It was just as bad trying to craftily sneak away for needed bathroom breaks....
Anyway, the purchased lunches were brought back to the pharmacy and

swiftly devoured while they resumed work, sometimes with mouths full of food. The delicatessen they frequented was the Jewish emporium right across East 86th Street, tucked in between the delipidated corner news stand and yet another knock-off of the original "Ray's" pizza parlor. The deli was authentically Kosher-inspired and called The Jewish Deli, with large numbers of cured sausages suspended from low-hanging rafters, the requisite pastrami odor in the air, and mean-looking, white-smocked, male personnel that seemed to perform as if part of a stereotypic condition of employment. Were they all "Soup Nazis," while dealing in meats, fish, and poultry in addition to soups? No, but most sure acted in a brusque and unfriendly manner as if trying hard to channel the city's gritty and no-nonsense vibe. However, my undeterred wife bought her midday meals there and summarily dismissed the false nastiness on display. The tasty and savory sliced cuts were fantastic, and you got tons for the price, so she kept returning in spite of the obnoxious *nudniks* who ran the place. And one of them was the owner, Moeshe. Hottie Blondie would order a giant, pastrami-packed, rye bread sandwich and then ask for a few extra pieces of bread with mayonnaise on them. In a thick Yiddish accent, Moeshe would explode in a mocking voice, "Listen lady, enjoy! You don't need to make ten more meals out of it!" My wife would uncharacteristically stand her ground and Moeshe would always relent and give her the extra rye slices and condiment toppings, complete with a wry smile from his garrulous face. It became a running joke between them for he knew that she would make extra sandwiches during her frenzied dinnertime at the pharmacy. I mean, how can you slam a pound of rich, salty, and flavorful meat at one sitting without falling asleep or suffering from indigestion afterwards? It was just too much at once, but Hottie Blondie knew how to handle it. Oftentimes she would even share her meaty good fortune with the others at the drugstore. After work she would occasionally patronize an official German deli down the street named Hasenpfeffer and load up on fresh ham, sauerkraut, and butter rolls to be eaten at frühstück (breakfast) the next morn. And the white-clothed, male, sour *Krauts* were the *wurst* and just as outwardly obstinate as the *schlubs* she encountered at the lunchtime Hebrew shop. In such a humongous metropolis, there was not a shortage of restaurants, eateries, cafes, and pull-carts from which to derive sustenance. The two she visited just happened to be conveniently located, although they were known to be on the expensive sides. However, the food products were top notch, as long as purchasers were aware of the caustic *shtick* that went along when buying them.

13

Bee-Bop-Barroob

Small groups of them would come in like clockwork, usually on a Friday evening, to stock up for the weekend. My wife would anticipate their arrival and be ready to direct them to the proper shelf for the outwardly innocuous cold product. However, arrogant R.K., her latest pharmacy partner, had not been privy to the "customary" end-of-the week happenings and was completely blindsided by this new, elderly trio. "Bee-Bop-Barroob," said the short and slightly built LatinX male to R.K., who stood behind the drug counter alongside Hottie Blondie.

"Bee-Bop-Barroob," the man repeated as his voice rose and his foreign-born buddies became visibly agitated. My wife stifled a laugh as R.K. stared at them blankly and held up his hands as if to say, "No comprende' and, what the fuck do you want?" The thickly accented catchphrase was uttered one more time before Hottie Blondie nonchalantly walked out to the tense motley crew and matter-of-factly found the prize for them. They smiled and thanked her immensely for helping them find their desired commodity. R.K.'s mouth dropped open as he watched the goings-on. "How did you know that Bee-Bop-Barroob meant Vick's Vapo Rub?" he hotly questioned my wife. "And are those guys really sick?" he further queried. Hottie

Blondie laughed and quipped that she just figured it out one day by trial and error. Furthermore, she explained that they most likely did not apply it to their respective torsos but rubbed it on their dicks as a stimulant before sex. At this point R.K. became visibly agitated and his eyes widened. How come HE didn't know about this street lingo and bizarre usage, yet my wife did? He always fancied himself as a *hip*, slang-aware pharmacist and did not appreciate Hottie Blondie having one over on him. Anyway, there were lots of creams and lotions boldly marketed and sold as counterirritants (rubefacients) for both sexes to be used as topical sex aids for the promotion of blood flow to erogenous zones. However, Vick's Vapo Rub was inexpensive and had no embarrassing stigma attached, especially when purchased in broad daylight from unaware pharmacy staff. Of course, Hottie Blondie had known that it was used for "other" purposes but was not one hundred percent sure. For all she knew, the malingering bunch of men that bought it had lingering colds and really did rub the cool, mentholated ointment on their hairy chests.

14

The Bernie Sandwich

Even though she grew up in the 'Dacks, Hottie Blondie never considered herself to be unsophisticated. Her previous five-year stint in pharmacy college only helped to solidify her self-confidence. In fact, working as a pharmacist in the heart of a big city made her believe that, although fairly young and newly married, she had already experienced much in life. Ha, ha. She was so unprepared for the Bernie sandwich! Back in the day, Bernie used to own and run his own drugstore in Brighton Beach, a small ethnic enclave of Brooklyn. Back then, pharmacy was a male-dominated profession; back before chains took over the business of pushing pills for people's ills. He was spry, wiry, gray-haired, and technically retired but worked the five to nine shift a few nights a week in the same drugstore as my wife. They got along great, although he was elderly, slow, and set in his pondering ways. But she enjoyed working alongside of him behind the drug bench during their brief overlaps on certain days. However, one evening she had to work a little later than usual to get caught up because of the days' overwhelming prescription load. And that's when shit hit the fan. She did not know that he took a hallowed time-out for dinner, and she unfortunately witnessed it in person. *Oy vey*, it was brutal. As she continued to hurriedly fill prescriptions, Hottie Blondie could not look away from the ritualized supper Bernie was preparing for himself. First, he laid out two big pieces of seeded, Jewish rye bread onto the sterile pharmacy counter. Then, he nonchalantly unwrapped a piece of newspaper which he had pulled from the same bag. He carefully unwrapped the soggy, printed paper and produced several, large, whole sardines that he ceremoniously and carefully lined up on the lower piece of rye. My wife instantly clamped her nose shut with her fingers in a mock response to the anticipated fishy odor and Bernie noticed. "Don't worry, they are fresh, I just got them from Feivel the Fishmonger this morning," he blandly insisted, as if it was common knowledge. And then Bernie continued with his culinary show: He reached down into his *Magic Bag*, much like Felix the Cat used to do, and produced a serrated knife plus a huge onion which he proceeded to cut into one-inch-thick slices, two of which he laid on his burgeoning Dagwood Bumstead-inspired work of gastronomical delight. Lastly came the giant wad of wet lettuce leaves that he dried with a paper towel and then piled over the onion pieces. There was no mayo, butter or other condiments used. It was just a jaw-breaking, sardine, raw onion, lettuce sandwich on rye, that's all! Are you kidding me? He had some nerve to create such a stank in the pharmacy. The fish-onion stench permeated the entire prescription area and Hottie

Blondie's eyes widened and reddened as he started noshing while she started to gag. Coming from the "mountains," she was used to the pungent scents of campfire smoke, Coyote urine, Mace bear spray, and industrial strength mosquito repellant. But even so, her keen sense of smell was violently violated by this seemingly innocuous sandwich. She wondered if he always ate "weird" foods like that. And did his breath reek as well? Bernie seemed to read her mind and stated that he grew up eating Yiddish dishes and this was nothing new to him. Now, my wife was a wizard in the kitchen and used plenty of garlic and onions to flavor the savory dishes she prepared at home. But never had she witnessed such epicurean audacity in a drugstore. But, then

again, this was the city and Bernie and
his ghastly grub most likely fit right in.

15

Riding the Rails

Hottie Blondie was pregnant, nauseous as hell, but still commuted to work every day as a loyal chain-store druggist. Plus, we needed the money because I was still a lowly and poorly paid dental resident at the local VA hospital. Sure, I had monetary PO-tential, but not quite yet. Anyhow, her frequent and long trips on the stinky, motion-sickness inducing F train made her feel awful. However, she knew it was caused by her "condition," so she bucked up, gritted her teeth, and swayed along with the jostling subway car that she was standing in. The lengthy rides back home were just as arduous. Couple that with the high crime rate that pervaded the city, and riding the rails was a cheap, but often unpleasant experience for the innocent populace involved. However, after lamenting her plight at her pharmacy, a young, handsome, Black, athletically built, store security guard showed some rare city-empathy and offered to shuttle home with her, at least up to his stop at Queens Boulevard. Actually, that was her last stop as well, before she boarded an overcrowded city bus on Woodhaven Boulevard for the remainder of her trek to our rental apartment on Doran Ave. But at least he was nice enough to accompany her most of the way home, and she was very grateful. However, sometimes things got a little uncomfortable during the homeward bound journeys, mostly because of her *Black Knight*. It seems that he fancied himself a bit of a player and played his hand to whichever cute Black chick was nearest him in the subway car. He assumed that no one paid any attention to the pregnant, White, blonde beauty standing right next to him, the one who leaned on him as the train lurched and swerved. He would continually chat up the surrounding ladies; some even reciprocated his heterosexual advances. They must have thought he was a virile, confident, and proven stud to flirt so openly in front of his expectant old lady. I mean, he had a gorgeous White gal knocked up and still had the *chutzpah* to brazenly ask for phone numbers right in front of her. And many were indeed given to him.

What a man, what a god! But some of the women questioned my wife if she was in fact his significant other and were disappointed when she said no. You know how it is: many cis-het females irrationally find committed men more irresistible than feckless bachelors. Anyway, whenever my wife would gently chide her "bodyguard," he sheepishly relented for a short while before resuming his womanizing ways. He told her that he could not help himself and they both laughed. In the end, Hottie Blondie was just happy that no one bothered her while being escorted by a "saintly" Casanova who flirtatiously took it all in stride.

16

Belly to Belly

A new pharmacy boss and another major headache. That was the essence of the latest debacle that befell my wife at her East 86th Street chain drugstore. She was the resident druggist, however, Jay B. was transferred to her store to replace the previous managing pharmacist. Unfortunately, that was not the obvious dilemma. The real problem was his abdominal heft versus her pregnancy belly! It was a daily comical interplay, at least that's how she initially described it. Jay B. was newly married to a carefully chosen nice Jewish girl. However, he was still a mamma's boy, and originally came from Crown

Heights, Queens. He was big and bold, and still retained that slight Yiddish accent from his childhood upbringing and neighborhood. And although fairly young, he already possessed a huge, overhanging paunch. In ancient times this would have signified male opulence and success. Nowadays, it basically denotes obesity. Anyway, there they were, polar opposites trying hard to meld as a pharmacy partnership. And then there were the petty, fleshy interactions between them. And, oh boy, it was not always pretty. Jay B. and my wife seemed to constantly "bump" their distended bellies together while running around to get the drug bottles off the shelves in the narrow spaces behind the cramped pharmacy counter. Hottie Blondie was slightly put out but chalked it up to the circumstances and never gave it a second thought. Whenever he "dry-humped" her while trying to sidle sideways behind her, she just lurched forward toward the drug bench a little so he could eventually pass. Well, those kinds of workplace shenanigans continued unabated until tech assistant and co-worker Kathy finally confided in her. "He constantly rubs against me too, and I'm not pregnant!" she lamented. Well, that was it. My wife was appalled and confronted Jay B. the next time he "innocently" squeezed past her. "That's quite enough, fat boy. No more belly rubs for you. And no more belly to belly or belly to BOTTOM!" she yelled out. Well, he got the message loud and clear. From that day forward he made

damn sure to avoid ANY physical
contact with Hottie Blondie, Kathy,
and other female assistants, probably
for fear of triggering a long overdue call
to HR.

17

Phony-Baloney

By now it may appear that Hottie Blondie was woefully unprepared not only for big city life, but also for the strain of working as a constantly harried pharmacist. But that was not entirely true. Although appearing timid in the face of manufactured adversity, she was in fact an outstanding druggist. However, though a self-effacing type of gal, even she had a boiling point. Her normal disposition was to let the usual drug-filling unpleasantries slide off her shoulders, but one thing really got her knickers in a twist. And that was phony prescriptions. One minute she was a good-natured and good-looking blonde, the next, a fuming flame of fury. How dare people bring in fake narcotic orders and try to hook her into filling them? Her moral compass, ethics, pharmacy scruples and very essence felt violated, dammit! Her inner demons were awakened and released whenever she was presented with bogus scripts. But, why? Who knows. Everyone has buttons that should not be pushed, and the unwary pushers often do so at their own peril. And such was the case with Hottie Blondie. There was a virtual "army" of conniving criminals and addicts who tried to twist the arms of unsuspecting druggists into illegally dispensing controlled substances. But she would have none of it. "But the other pharmacist filled it!" was a common refrain. "I get it here all the time, what's the problem?" was also a familiar and sarcastic rejoinder. However, the fakery came in differing flavors: Sometimes the paper prescriptions themselves, like "funny money," were inauthentic with a fictitious doctor's name, address, DEA number, etc. Sometimes the scripts were genuine but were stolen from a careless prescriber's office. Other times a doctor had been duped and even though the prescription was "legal," either the amount of drug, the high dosage involved, or frequency with which it was to be filled made it appear highly dubious. However, sometimes a legitimate practitioner was in cahoots with the receiver of said medicine. There could be drug or monetary kickbacks involved in a sophisticated scheme of collusion, all for the sake of peddling certain medications to hapless addicts. Nevertheless, there were also times when a doctor's office, most likely for monetary reasons, became well known as an illicit pill-prescribing center with no morals or medical conscience. You want it? You got it – and pay cash as you exit! Thusly, my wife was always on the lookout for all the aforementioned ways to procure the Percodan, so to speak. Even so, the ensuing furtive phone calls to physician offices, patient demands and denials, and resulting threatening arguments were draining and stressful. Some patients immediately walked out when sensing that Hottie Blondie was on to them. Others knew the jig was up but continued to aggressively berate her out of frustration. Still others patiently waited while she jumped through hoops checking on the validity of the prescription in hopes that she would give up after wasting so much time and just dispense it to them. Ha, ha, no can do! But the upshot was that whenever my wife spoke up and reminded her co-workers, technicians and partner pharmacist about this scourge of phony-baloney, she was often met with glazed-over stares and an attitude of ambivalence. The hired hands knew who most of the scruffy repeat offenders were and from which parts of the city many of the fraudulent prescriptions came from. But they apparently did not care. "Why rock the boat?" seemed to be the laissez-faire drugstore mantra. And even if there were suspicions of trickery going on, only Hottie Blondie stepped up to the plate and valiantly tried to do the right thing. The other employees basically stepped off at the first sign of trouble, with the excuse being that the pharmacy would not be held liable because it was hard to catch deception. Really? Anyway, my wife's messianic fervor probably did virtually nothing to stem the pharmaceutical threats of overprescribing, overusing and abusing. As long as there were "complicit" pharmacists behind the bench who willingly dispensed hard drugs, nothing could be done to at least put a damper on the resultant "legalized" drug trade.

18

Locked In

Being locked out of the house or car are both unfortunate and nerve-wracking events that can happen to anyone. But what about being locked in and unable to vacate the premises? That's right, Hottie Blondie hurriedly scurried around at the last moments, still filling prescriptions and getting the new and cumbersome computer system to shut down properly. Then she collected her personal belongings and went to the bathroom one last time after finally finishing the demanding evening shift. It was just after 9 p.m. and all she wished to do was get the hell out of the drugstore and hopefully, survive yet another nightly trip to her house without being assaulted, mugged or killed. All she wanted was to go home. But she couldn't. It seems that in the typical mad rush of departing employees, the new front-store manager had forgotten about her while she was quietly fritzing around behind the pharmacy counter. He had set the alarms, locked the glass front door, and taken off. Eventually Hottie Blondie approached that very door but could not budge it. And come to think of it, there were no people around. The store was eerily quiet, too quiet. The lights were on but there was nobody home! Crap, she was locked in and could not exit. She was hungry, tired, and now, really pissed off. How dare that manager NOT check on her, especially after she did the drugstore a favor by staying late to finish the deluge of prescriptions that had crazily backed up during the afternoon. Well, she had done the pharmacy a solid but now found herself solidly locked up. However, she knew enough about the security system and, without tripping it, carefully tiptoed back to the pharmacy department to make some phone calls from the land line. This was way before cellphones, mind you. The first call went to the manager's house phone, but he did not pick up because he was still on his way there. The second call went to 911. The police quickly arrived with squad car sirens blaring and lights a-winking. You know, a tactical response to a possible 10-31 (crime in progress). But before shots were fired or a battering ram utilized, an officer with half a brain decided to first call the store. Hottie Blondie answered and explained the whole fucked-up situation. Then the very gravid, blonde hottie calmly walked to the front door and revealed herself as a white-coated, badged, and official druggist to an army of ogling armed coppers. At this point she was no longer concerned about triggering the store alarms and relaxed a bit. Through primitive sign language, she "told" the *Fuzz* that as soon as she was able to get ahold of the manager - who had the only key - he would come and let her out. A police officer was then positioned outside the storefront to periodically wave and check on her as the rest of the Men in Blue reluctantly departed. But it was getting very late when she decided to call me, AFTER she had eventually contacted that boneheaded manager. I had been worried sick and did not know what to do up until she, like E.T., phoned home. I quickly jumped into my trusty klunker - which had been previously stored for years at my folks' house - and floored it out of our quiet and genteel Italian neighborhood in Glendale, Queens. There was no way I would let her ride the trains this late at night. I would be there within the hour and drove that car like a madman - you know, just like most of the city drivers did on any normal day. Meanwhile, her hunger pangs increased exponentially, being pregnant and all. While normally a gentle soul, she was mad that night,

and starving. She grabbed a large
Snickers bar, angrily tore open the
cellophane covering, wolfed it down,
and did not pay for it! "Fuck them for
locking me in," she uncharacteristically
reasoned and then reached out for a
giant Baby Ruth bar. That was her
dinner as she washed down the candy
treats with a Yoo-hoo chocolate drink,
which she also considered a tin roof
– you know, "on the house." In the
meantime, our unborn child was doing
somersaults and backflips because of
the sudden and unexpected sugar high
she received. Anyhow, all ended well.
Just as I pulled up to the curb, the
flustered and chagrined store manager
arrived to extricate my wife from her
involuntary incarceration. The smiling
cop waved goodbye as the sniveling

manager profusely apologized. Hottie Blondie and I kissed and held each other tightly. Oh, well, it was just another screwed-up situation but par for the course and yet another notch in my wife's lipstick case (thank you Pat Benatar), a case of leftover naïveté that would soon be replaced with a cagier approach to pharmacy, and life in general.

19

Bombs Again?

No chain-store druggist ever needed any extra aggravation, but unnecessary bullshit kept right on coming. You know how it is. For example, when my wife was nearing the end of her pregnancy, the bomb threats called into her store on East 86th Street kept increasing. First it was monthly, then weekly, and then almost daily. What the hell? She was ready to pop and definitely not in the mood for this kind of added malarkey. Whomever fielded the threatening phone calls would report it through the customary chain of command, and then the usual protocols would be followed: A telephone call placed to the same bomb squad unit at the local police department, followed by a temporary evacuation order of all patients and shoppers, and then locking the front door until the coast was clear. It was all so silly, but necessary because you never knew if and when it would be real. Anyway, the special-forces cops, who were encased in head-to-toe, shrapnel-proof zoot-suits along with their bomb-detecting dogs, would arrive and canvas the exterior and interior of the drugstore. All the while the exposed and lightly dressed pharmacy staff would stand numbly by, watching the repeat performances. Hottie Blondie would always get majorly annoyed whenever the dumb dogs would illegally go behind the "sterile" counter

and sniff her up while their armor-clad
male owners gave her the once over
with leering looks. And then she had to
go outside, ignominiously sit inside a
police cruiser, be sternly interviewed as
if a suspected criminal, and fill out an
incident report for the umpteenth time!
Oh well, no bombs were ever
discovered ticking behind the Tampax
boxes or inside the Trojans
prophylactics display. Or in the staff
restroom or outside dumpster, for that
matter. It was all an expensive joke
perpetrated by some sociopathic psycho
who got her jollies from causing
mayhem and terror. Yet sometimes my
wife's pregnancy caused her to have
hormonally induced morbid thoughts,
such as wishing that the prank caller
had indeed planted a legitimate

explosive device; one that would've blown the whole damn place to smithereens and ended everyone's "suffering" once and for all. Those macabre thoughts were fleeting and thank goodness, nothing happened. The bomb scares had been a cat and mouse game that eventually faded without the responsible *rascally rodent* ever being caught. But it really didn't matter. Tomorrow there would be another unplanned-for and unpleasant fiasco. As Roseanne Roseannadanna of SNL-fame would say, "It's always something." Anyhow, Hottie Blondie was ready to quit anyway and to give birth, in that order. And she did both.

20

Happy and Gay

My wife, toddler daughter, and I were excited to finally and fully transition - not sexually - from city inhabitants to suburbanites, and then once more, to *country bumpkins*. Although Hottie Blondie was originally from the Adirondacks, and I from the Catskills, our mutual pharmacy college in the state's capital had been the marriage broker that facilitated our nuptials. And, so, we temporarily returned to the scene of the crime. We settled on one side of a duplex rental building in a decent neighborhood while our custom home was being built a bit farther north in an area designated as rural residential. A place where gunshots were heard regularly, but they came from hunters and not hoodlums. And instead of being raised as a quintessential "Queens Girl" (a derisive moniker given to the big-haired and hair-brained female city teenagers back in the '80s), my daughter, and later son, would grow up on a dead-end street, on 3.16 acres of land, with a man-made pond in the backyard next to a mini forest, and a huge, green lawn to play on. *Rednecksville*, baby! Nearby neighbors were not nosy and barely visible through the thick tree lines that bordered our adjacent and respective properties. I was an associate dentist on the verge of buying a large and lucrative dental practice in a nearby city and my wife thought she'd contribute by working at least two days per week, when I would be available to babysit our child. So, she made a concerted effort to get hired on a part-time basis at a local drugstore. And she made it happen. Wednesdays and Saturdays would be her pharmacist days, plus a few evenings per week, in a puny, privately-owned, retail setting. It was part of a tiny, L-shaped, strip-mall right down the street from where we were renting – bonus! Hottie Blondie was happy; the couple who owned the drugstore were happy… and gay. Though on a serious note, neither were druggists and in New York State, only a duly licensed pharmacist can own a pharmacy. Somehow the State never checked on the status of that store…. Anyhow, Hottie Blondie did not care and absolutely loved her employment. The hands-on owners handled the cash box, inventory, and finances and got on famously with their new, hot, blonde recruit. Although there were "reliable" rumors whispered about him, she never did meet the supposedly crabby old druggist who worked the other days of the week. The store had no assistants, save for the two male lovebirds, and she ran the big show solo from behind the elevated counter. It reminded her of her father's small pharmacy where he was the big boss, in addition to his bossy manager wife and two bossy female clerks. But here there were no self-important chieftains or petulant patients. The customers were mostly cordial, and the overall working atmosphere was delightful. She could have made twice as much money working for a chain outfit again, but why? She was enjoying life, her chosen profession, and our young daughter while I was gradually getting in gear as a potentially successful prosthodontist. I also had great times with my mini-me, budding-naturalist offspring. I would belt her into the stroller and together we traversed the many deserted side-streets in our neighborhood 'burbs, always on the look-out for "voles and weasels." Then we would hit the local playground, but her idea of fun was to explore nature instead of playing on the slides and swings. We would also frequently drive up to visit our property in the wilderness and, besides catching *bugs and slugs* there, watched as our new domicile was being completed.

Eventually, it was time to relocate. Just after my wife birthed a son, we expectantly moved into our new digs in the "country." Hottie Blondie said a tearful goodbye to probably the most relaxed and rewarding pharmacy practice she had ever dispensed drugs in. And she cried again in front of two grown men who had affectionately grown on her and had truly made that brief pharmacy adventure so exceptional.

21

Night Moves

It had been a staple song played repeatedly on the corner jukebox in our favorite dive bar during Hottie Blondie's and my five-year pharmacy college journeys. And that 1976 Bob Seger track was appropriately played at night, when pharmacy students from all class years would gather in the off-campus, unofficial "student union" on the corner of Madison and New Scotland Avenues. It was a grungy place, but nonetheless a revered spot where like-minded future druggists mingled, sought out potential partners, played foosball, drank, and had a few laughs. Needless to say, Hottie Blondie and I started going steady and became steady fixtures at that dinky, alcoholic emporium…. Anyway, fast forwarding about two decades found my wife, still the one and only Hottie Blondie and now the mother of two, working part time for a multiple chain drugstore in the western Capital District area. Not simply as a super floater daytime pharmacist, but also as a substitute druggist during the graveyard shift. However, her new night moves were no longer imbibing, *inhaling*, and mating with her college boyfriend, the eccentric, eclectic, and notorious party animal known as The Smallman (me). No, Hottie Blondie's newest job oftentimes consisted of filling scripts throughout the nighttime in dingy 24-hour drugstores located in some of

the filthiest and seediest places in
Skankectady. But it had been HER
choice of chain pharmacies to work for,
and to be "chained to the bench" at
dusk whenever she was needed in a
pinch. With her children basically
grown and having an actively engaged
dentist husband, she thought that
sporadically practicing at night could
not only earn her a few Benjamins, but
would also allow her the luxury of
spending quality daytime hours on
previously neglected hobbies and
personal interests. You know, trying to
burn the candle at both ends and
hoping for a happy middle. Well, it
didn't work out as planned. It was
tough being "on call" and then
frantically phoned by frazzled pharmacy
managers and coerced into accepting

assignments last minute. But the real madness of the situation was the job itself. Much like the mob of unsavory characters from the original 1980's TV sitcom *Night Court*, the *creatures* that emerged and frequented a drugstore in the wee hours were, for the most part, not exactly prime human specimens. Oh, there were legit emergency prescriptions brought in by ill people or the occasional blurry-eyed insomniacs who dropped by for their Sominex or Unisom. However, by and large it was the unwashed weirdos, junkies, and lonely, dirty old men who sometimes made Hottie Blondie's workplace an uncomfortable den of inequity with lascivious undertones. Many of the *miscreants* just wanted to stay warm and shoot the shit while slowly sucking a soda or chewing on a "freebie" Slim Jim. However, she concomitantly felt "assaulted," both visually and auditorily. In return, she had to judiciously watch her mannerisms, be on the lookout for would-be troublemakers, and be very careful when articulating to the real *creepy crawlers*. And most of all, just to stay awake! She eventually realized that operating in the darkness was doing a number on her. Really? Duh! All that circadian and biorhythm mumbo jumbo seemed to be correct after all. Hottie Blondie would come home exhausted and needed at least forty-eight hours to reset her inner mental clock, physical countenance, and come to her senses. Additionally, she was basically useless as a parent and sexual participant during those two "recovery" days. Unlike pharmacists that were conditioned to the third shift, working it infrequently was traumatic for both her body and mind. Hottie Blondie ended up quitting that "nerve-wrecking" job AND the chain company. She had suddenly seen enough and started to seriously consider retirement, at least from pharmacy.

22

Fighting the Good Fight

She was officially licensed, hitched to a dental resident, living in a cockroach overrun rental apartment, and all set to optimistically conquer the world as a wildly busy, chain-store pharmacist on East 70th Street. Really? That seemingly full plate was already on the noggin of an anxious 22-year-old, yet, it was just the beginning of a torturous journey, one where she would be forced to tackle far more than pills and potions. For instance, the unrelenting and deafening cacophony of trains, buses, honking cabs, and general city noise continually played upon her unseasoned hearing. Combine that with the unrelenting stress caused by high-strung humans and street crime, which was ubiquitous and deemed normal, and Dorothy was no longer in Kansas! Nevertheless, Hottie Blondie successfully battled back all the pharmaceutical and surrounding foes thrown her way. She then moved to Queens and unfortunately braved a long and danger-filled commute to a new, but similarly hellish drugstore on East 86th Street, in the same unholy metropolis. Shortly after giving birth to a genetic female, the whole family got the hell out of Dodge in a goddamn hurry. Almost immediately after her husband had completed his prosthodontic specialty residency program, they strapped themselves into their olive green 1970 Plymouth Valiant, got onto the Major Deegan

Expressway at midnight, and hightailed it North like a bat out of hell (thank you Meatloaf)! They settled in bucolic upstate New York near the familiar state capital, and Hottie Blondie found employment in a wonderful, small, private pharmacy owned by a male gay couple. However, neither were pharmacists and the ownership was considered illegal under state law. Oh, well. While relatively short-lived, it turned out to be a satisfying experience and enabled Hottie Blondie to continually contribute to her young family's coffers. However, after birthing another child, this time a biological male, she decided to join the *chain gang* one more time, but as a super floater and substitute pharmacist. Her prosthodontist husband had started to make bank as a dental practice owner and the onus on her as the majority family breadwinner greatly diminished. Nevertheless, even her part-time hours were fucked with. Additionally, she disliked working the night shift or being sent to skeevy areas. Suddenly she found herself "fighting" again, just like she did years ago, and finally got sick of it. So, she abjectly, prematurely, and politely retired. The famously recited movie line, "What's a nice girl like you doing in a place like this?" was very applicable to Hottie Blondie throughout most of her professional retail career. She had tried the best she could, but at the end there was no love lost between her and her last employer. Although there was the possibility of other pharmacy-related employment opportunities, she determined that any earned *shekels* were no longer a requirement for her family's finances. In hindsight, it's fitting to quote *Fight the Good Fight*, a 1981 power-ballad by the Canadian rock-trio, Triumph. In the lyrics of that most excellent song is a line that reads: "it's your only way." And that one sentence aptly summed up Hottie Blondie's retail pharmacy career. She fought hard daily because it was *her only way*. Nonetheless, it's most unfortunate that the word fight was so often used in her vocabulary during her working years, especially when employed by the chain drugstores. And even though now long retired, it still tellingly escapes her mouth whenever she chooses to discuss her former

profession with uninitiated and
uninformed hoi polloi.

23

Please, Allow Me:

Pharmacy is a necessary and noble profession, so why did this book seem to accentuate the cringeworthy under the guise of humor? But au contraire - it was written with the best of intentions and in the spirit of good fun. In other words, I sought to expose the WHOLE world of retail pharmacy, warts and all. There was no axe to grind; I went from counting pills to counting teeth, remember? Nevertheless, at least two things continue to chafe me. First, let's briefly discuss pharmacy education. My beloved father-in-law, Joe (ACPHS '61), attended pharmacy college for FOUR years; my wife, younger sister, and I for FIVE years apiece. Nowadays, instead of a B.S., you receive a PharmD after SIX years of effort. Do you see where this is heading? It seems as if the pharmacy profession has quietly been hijacked, hoodwinked, and hornswoggled by a cabal of liberal elites in higher education, ones that have their sights set on an even longer tenure for hapless pharmacy students. But, why? And what's next? Will a four-year prepharmacy program followed by four years of pharmaceutical sciences and then a residency suffice? Holy tuition increase, Batman! And what will the new, EIGHT-plus-year degree be called – a Pharm Double D? Good Lord, talk about being overly well-endowed. Give me a fuckin' break. Now, if students want to become scientists, industry-researchers, or professors then, yes, the more "learning" the better. However, what about the *mensches* who wish to work in the trenches and earn a reasonable buck? With the sophistication of computers, technology, and technicians in most modern-day drugstores, there is no need for dispensing druggists to be overly educated! If the objective is to "work the bench" at a Consumer Value Store (CVS), then there is a serious disconnect between present-day pharmacy education and retail reality. Thusly, is a one-size-fits-all college curriculum still appropriate and valid? I don't think so. Instead, two graduation tracks could be instituted – a retail arm, and one for industry, research, and science. But don't hold your breath for that to happen. My second major gripe, and I'm almost finished now, is the misguided notion that retail pharmacists want to do more at work. Really? Who said? Bamboozled and bushwhacked again, I'm afraid! But this time by the cabal of corporate elites. Sadly, "playing doctor," giving injections, viral testing, being a health insurance wizard, and counseling patients up the wazoo are extra-curriculars that are now considered the norm. It was supposedly done to fulfill the needs and desires of a restive, unappreciative, ambivalent, yet demanding public. And, of course, for the extra moolah generated. Yet, at no significant renumeration or added prestige for the pharmacist, mind you.

WTF, is this the newest rat race and jonesing? Drugstore chains constantly trying to up the ante and OUTSHINE one another by tasking the rank and file to do ever more for less? Wow, what a bunch of *Shinola!* In conclusion, and in my humble opinion, today's intelligent cadre of retail druggists are quite possibly overeducated, overtrained, and overworked, period.

Thank you for allowing me this seemingly unseemly digression.

24

Disclaimer for Retail Pharmacists

I sincerely hope you will have, or have had, a long and satisfying career in retail pharmacy. To that end, I am profoundly sorry if I inadvertently vilified innocent individuals, fellow druggists, and the pharmacy profession in general. It was unintentional, although collateral verbal damage can occur when writing from dusty and possibly distorted memories. I successfully graduated from pharmacy college, fulfilled my internship, externship, and licensing requirements, then worked as a druggist for a few summers during my dental school tenure. Because of my brief foray into pharmacy, I never succumbed to the unbelievably stressful and "mind-numbing" retail careers of most of my former college peers. And that reality includes my father-in-law, wife, and younger sister, who all diligently plugged away as long-term retail pharmacists with nary a whimper heard.

25

Last Words

With my wife's immeasurable help, I wrote this book not as a vengeful diatribe, but to poke a little fun at the *conscious uncoupling* that occurs between what most retail pharmacists are taught and how they end up practicing. Also, I wanted to highlight some of the ridiculous and hilarious events that were foisted upon my wife and me during our pharmacy careers. Sure, there were genuinely lighthearted moments here and there, but most of the heinous working days were bereft of honest humor. In addition, whenever unplanned and surprisingly comical situations arose, they often did so at the expense of the druggist or patient. But wait a minute, pharmacy is not supposed to be an inherently funny profession, or is it? Anyway, hopefully the slightly jaded reflections of two former pharmacists brought out some heartfelt guffaws.

My wife and I became pharmacists for "duty and humanity," a seminal line lifted from the medically themed, 1934 Three Stooges short *Men in Black*. And like that comedic episode illustrates, having a sense of humor, no matter the dire circumstances or vocation, is an invaluable skill to possess. It greatly helped my wife as she ably navigated her pharmacy career while working for the *chain gang* and beyond. Congrats to Hottie Blondie for having made it to the finish line with her funny bone intact and without obvious signs of PTSD (Pharmacist Traumatic Stress Disorder), although….

Thanks for the read.

About the Authors

Dr. I Mayputz (not his real name) graduated with highest honors from high school, pharmacy college, and summa cum laude from dental school. After completing a master's degree in prosthodontics at a then-prestigious institution, he embarked on his dental career in private practice. He is now retired. As an elite Master's athlete, he has won various championships in singles tennis, sprinting, snow-shoe sprinting, javelin and singles pickleball. In addition to being a verbal artist, naturalist, and part-time naturist, he is also known as a caustic wit and provocateur. Dr. I. Mayputz has previously published comedy novels using his pseudonym as well as released numerous nature articles in regional journals under his real name. Additionally, he has authored multiple scholarly pharmaceutical and dental abstracts and written many children's books, also under his given name. Lastly, he wrote this book to entertain family, old friends, college alumni, and any curious sod willing to experience *life* as a retail pharmacist.

Mrs. I. Mayputz (not her real name) graduated with highest honors from high school and pharmacy college. She began her chosen profession as a chain-store druggist, taking time out to raise her two children. After a distinguished career as a well-respected pharmacist, she happily retired. In addition to her current part-time job of substance abuse and gambling addiction recovery coaching, she is also known for her beauty, superb pickleball abilities, culinary magic, advanced Reiki skills, and keen sense of humor. After all, she has managed to stay married to that *putz* Dr. I. Mayputz for over four decades! She contributed most of the stories for this book which her husband faithfully transcribed, although in his quirky, acerbic, and debauched style.

For more alleged levity by Dr. I. Mayputz, please read:

Dental School: A Bizarre Comedy

Pharmacy College: Crazy Daze and Hazy Nites

Elementary School: Wits and Twits

Junior High: The Muddle Years

High School: Buffoonery Central

Dental Delirium: A "Humorous" Look at Dentistry

Retired… And I'm Still Tired!

www.ingramcontent.com/pod-product-compliance
Lightning Source LLC
Chambersburg PA
CBHW022007120726
47992CB00001B/448